Clint Faraday
book forty five
Death Doesn't Wait

Omar is in the cantina talking with a semi-pretty hippie type girl who seems a bit spaced out. She writes weird poetry and likes adventure. She is going kite riding tomorrow.

Omar says that's not safe along the coast. She could end up a bloody mess on the rocks.

She replies that everybody dies sometime.

He says he'll delay death as long as he can.

She says, "When your time comes, you die. Death doesn't wait for anyone".

It certainly didn't wait for her.

Contents

About the author

CD Moulton has traveled extensively over much of the world both in the music business, where he was a rock guitarist, songwriter and arranger and in an import/export business. He has been everything from a bar owner to auto salvage (junkyard) manager, longshoreman to high steel worker, orchid grower to landscaper, tropical fish farmer to commercial fisherman. He started writing books in 1983 and has published more than 350 books as of January 1, 2023. His most popular books to date are about research with orchids, though much of his science fiction and fantasy work has proven popular. He wrote the CD Grimes, PI series, and the Det. Nick Storie series, Clint Faraday series, and many other works.

He now resides in Gualaca, Chiriqui, Panamá, where he writes books, plays music with friends, does research with orchids and medicinal plants. He has lately become involved in fighting for the rights of the indigenous people, who are among his closest friends, and in fighting the extreme corruption in the courts and police in Panamá.

He offers the free e-book, *Fading Paradise*, that explains what he has been through because of the corruption.

CD is the discoverer of the Chadam Protocol for curing cancer.

Facebook page Ambrosia peruviana for cancer.

Omar Estevez looked at the almost pretty gringa reading a poem she wrote and shook his head.

"The clouds surround me and are part of me. -
The wind encompasses my body in dreams. -
I float. -
The world comes to me in song. -
I ... I can't find the right word, but 'exhilarate' might fit ... in fantasy and thought.
Then I do not think any more. -
Life surrounds me, becomes me. -
I wonder at the world and it wonders at me. -
This is peace. This is plenty. -
I awaken refreshed and alive and happy.

"I don't much care for that last line. This is just an idea. I have to work on it more. Words aren't as easy to use as one would prefer. A syllable can destroy art.

"I'll have another red wine, please ... oh! Una mas vino tinta, por favor!

"Harry isn't here? We're supposed to go kiting tomorrow. I don't know if he was able to get the boat."

She walked to the little shelf that served as a bar

and Sareta poured her a small glass of Close. She smiled at Omar and said, "I'm Sandra Miller. Call me Sandy. I'm a poet and adventuress. Very good at both.

"I suppose you don't speak English, but that was a poem I'm working on."

"I speak some English. Omar Estevez, typical Indio bum, but a fantastic lover. That's what I'm good at, but I also fish and make jewelry from the natural things here."

"You, I like! No shit and no line that I've heard a thousand times. You're very handsome. A lot of the Indios are. Yes, I'll sleep with you tonight. This is a vacation. I don't play games in my head. I want sex with a stranger, preferably an Indio. It's part of an exotic vacation."

"You are going kiting tomorrow? You will be pulled with the boat with that parachute thing on a rope?"

"Yes. I want to get some pictures from a new perspective. I've taken some from underwater – you were about to tell me I have to land in the water and it would ruin the camera – with this camera. It's a Stylus. It can be used in the water or on land."

"That thing is dangerous on the coast here. You could end up a bloody mess on the rocks."

"When your time comes, you die. Death doesn't

wait for anyone. I'll die doing what I like.

"You smoke weed?"

"Not very much. It doesn't affect me the way it does some people. It just makes me sleepy. It's good when you have a headache or nausea."

"Take off your shirt."

"What?"

"You have a beautiful body. I want my friends to see it and be jealous because I got the best one here."

He shrugged and took off the shirt. He really was well-built. That's true of most Indios of his age (24) on the comarcas. He'd been working since he was seven or eight years old and part of the family system, carrying things and digging and swimming. At ten he was able to do work that most gringos eighteen couldn't do.

He also liked sex and was a very good lover. He didn't play games with these gringas who came specifically to get laid.

"I'm not the best one here, but thanks. I mean to look at. Esteban and Andres are better looking, but I'm a better lover. Ask anyone!"

She laughed. "You mean those two dolls? (She pointed). Should I ask them if you're the best lover?"

He wasn't going to let her get one up on him with that, so he looked innocent and replied,

"Why not?"

She looked confused, then grinned. "I'll bet you would! A friend who was here last year is gay and said he never had so much really good sex anywhere in his life.

"Do you?"

"What?"

"Screw guys."

"Sure. Everyone does. We just don't lie about it."

"Which means they screw you?" She had a devilish grin on her face.

"Turn about's fair play."

"Now I don't know if you're putting me on!"

"A little. I have and they have and will again.

"You had enough wine?"

"Yeah! Let's hit the sack! I think it's going to be a great night!"

They went up to her hotel room. It was a great night for both of them except when Gina Berts stormed into the room and called her a sick sneaky bitch – and leave Harry alone! He was with her!

"Yeah! And you're going to sleep with that Indio tonight and Harry's going to sleep with an Indian woman. I'm sleeping with the best I've ever had and George will be sleeping with whoever has the time. It's a vacation, for Christ's sake! Have some fun! Don't get to feeling guilty and take it out on me!

"Go to bed! You get a few beers in you and turn into a silly harpy."

She slammed back out. Omar and Sandy got back to what they were doing.

In the morning Sandy went to the dock and got on the boat with a gringo and Max, who owned the boat. There were six other gringos there, but they wouldn't go out in the boat, though they were all in and around it until it left.

Clint Faraday, retired PI from Florida, who was now living in Panamá, was by the dock when Omar brought Sandy. He was introduced to the group and was talking with Omar as the boat left the dock. Matilde, the local medicine woman and witch (not the evil kind) came to stare at the boat. She turned to Clint and said (in the dialect), "One will not return. It is a very evil deed. It is a very evil person. The spirit. The body will look like a friend, but the spirit is evil and has no friends. That spirit will not return here."

She walked away. Clint knew she wouldn't say more. He also knew one of them wouldn't be coming back. Matilde was never wrong.

He and Omar went to his boat to get some things he'd brought from Chiriqui Grande. He would take the tools and supplies to his place, about a kilometer up the beach where his wife, Tyna, and two children, Nito and Nicole, were staying. He'd brought the children to the school he'd built there in Cusapín.

Omar told Clint about the crazy spaced-out chick, Sandy, and last night.

"We were honest with each other. I hope it was not her Matilde was talking about. I don't think she's evil."

Clint nodded. They carried the items to his house and gave them to Tyna to do what she wanted with, then headed back toward the town.

They were almost there when Omar spotted the kite boat down near the point.

"I wish he wouldn't go so close to the rocks. The wind swirls there when it's from the east."

Just about then they saw one of the two kites being pulled along spin. The one side seemed to tear loose from the ropes and was flapping. The person who was riding was trying desperately to drop toward the water slowly instead of in a plunge.

They were close to the point east. The wind was from the east. The kite plunged down.

From the distance they couldn't tell how far out the boat was from the rocks. They might have been farther than it seemed and it would be alright. The rider would hit the water.

They heard a very faint scream, then shouts.

"Well, Matilde was, as always, right. I wonder which one's spirit will not be coming back," Omar said.

Clint watched as they brought the body of Sandra Miller to the dock. She had dropped into the rocks at the point when the lower winds twisted her back that way. Max said the rope from the stabilizer broke. He couldn't figure it. It was new polypropylene and wouldn't break before it pulled the entire transom off the boat – and the transom was welded!

Clint checked the rope. It had been hardened somehow. Max was crying that he couldn't see how such an accident could happen. He took perfect care of his equipment!

"It didn't," Clint said, dryly. "It wasn't an accident. It was murder."

"Murder!?" a man who was watching cried. "She ... I mean ... You have to be wrong!"

"Maybe it was only intended to scare her, but it happened too close to those rocks," Clint replied. "The rope had a very hardened spot right by the transom hook. The wind twists hard at the point trying to come from two directions when it's from the east. The hardened spot would have no sheer strength, so snapped. The wind pushed her south, then spun her east and over the rocks.

"If just scaring her was the object, it's still murder."

The man went to the group who were traveling with Sandy and told them what Clint said.

Naldo Flores, a friend, came to say that Basilio was in Chiriqui Grande and had requested that Clint investigate whatever needed investigating for the council. Clint agreed. He said Naldo and Omar could act as assistants if they would. Naldo said he would and Omar said he would do all he could, but he had to go fishing tomorrow.

They went to the little council house and Clint called the police in Chiriqui Grande and asked that they cooperate by supplying information. He had reached some woman who was new. She said he would have to go through normal channels to get police information sent to the comarca. The police in the towns were not stationed there for the convenience of the comarcas. If they had the time, they would look for the information and send it.

"Then you can tell Capitan Generoso we will be holding all gringos or other tourists in the jail in Cusapín until my investigation is completed and they have been cleared. I don't understand why this sudden attitude. The police here have always responded very well to the council." He hung up before she could say anything.

Omar grinned. Naldo laughed. Clint counted, "...seven, six, five, four, three, two, one!" and pointed to the phone. It rang about five seconds later.

"Basilio? What in hell's going on! Why have you declared we can't come to the comarca to investigate something or other?"

"Hi, Generoso. It's Clint. I asked for some information and got a silly lecture about police cooperating with the Indios at *your* option not *ours*. I told her we'd keep all the tourists here in jail until we had the information in that case.

"She new?"

"Very. What do you need?"

"We have a bit of a murder. A tourist girl by the name of Sandra Miller. Very obviously, no one on the comarca would have a reason to kill anyone from outside in such a way. My suspects are the tourists.

"She seemed alright. Rather typical, but Matilde took one look and said she had an evil spirit and that she would go out in the boat, but the spirit wouldn't return. After the boat had left the dock."

"Matilde? Oh, holy shit!" Everyone knew that Matilde was never wrong.

Clint would check everyone and would send the passport information. Generoso would check out everyone.

Clint told Naldo to go to the dock and make it plain that no one was to leave until they'd been checked and cleared. Ten minutes later four very angry people charged into the room.

"We have to be in Bocas tomorrow! You can't hold us here!" one of the men yelled.

"You are?" Clint asked.

"I'm Jim Burrows. I know my rights! You can't keep me here! I didn't even *know* the dead broad before!"

"Then a few questions and that will be shown and there's no reason to get your shorts in a knot, right?" Clint asked, reasonably. Burrows turned redder than he was and mumbled something.

"I'm Jennifer Clift. *You* may call me *Miss* Clift. I am not going to answer any questions until my lawyer is present. I know my rights, too, you see!"

"Where the hell do you think you are? Miami?" Omar asked. "You don't have any rights here that Clint don't give you. This is the comarca."

"Let's not let this get out of hand. You get your hackles up for the damnedest reasons, Jenny! I was told that the laws don't apply on the comarcas – it says that right there in the guide, Jenny!"

"I'm Lily Owens. This is Sam Keys. What do you want to know?"

"The dead girl's name was Sandra Miller. She

was from Vermont. She was twenty four years old. She was a poet and backpacker on a lark," Clint said. "Did you know her or anyone in her group before here?"

"We've been together ever since we met in Managua, Nicaragua, three weeks ago. We went to Costa Rica, but there were no waves so we came here. Bocas. They told us about this place and we came to see it. We did some surfing and met them in that little restaurant place where she picked up her boyfriend there." She pointed to Omar, who grinned. She grinned back. "She read some bad poetry, but she seemed a regular type of the hippie crowd. We met them, where was it, Sam? On the point?"

"Yeah. About eleven yesterday morning. Some good waves for practice. We talked and went to the restaurant with them last night.

"She seemed to have some kind of personal problem with that Gina girl. You could tell they didn't like each other."

"I heard her say Sandy was an evil bitch when Sandy was talking to Harry. I think Gina was with Harry and Sandy was trying to cut in or something. They aren't promised or anything, so why get all hot about it?

"I may have seen some of them at conventions or somewhere. I don't know. Sandy may have been at the one in San Diego, California."

"Gina was the one who came into the room last night and said Sandy was trying to fuck Harry. Sandy said she was with me so that was bullshit. Harry would sleep with whoever he wanted and she would sleep with Andres or something," Omar said.

"She said you told her you were the best lover here and that she agreed you were the best she ever had," Sam said.

"Well, Naldo will take your passport information and Omar can get the others to come in. Maybe I'll be able to spot something," Clint said. "I think I can get all I need about you this afternoon and you can go on to Bocas on schedule – unless you killed her. We frown on that kind of thing here on the comarca."

They laughed. Jenny Clift apologized for being a bitch when they came in. She said she was scared shitless because she had pot in her bag, but that wasn't illegal on the comarca was it?

"Like anything else, don't let it interfere with others and nobody cares," Omar said. They all left. Omar sent the passport information on to Generoso, then went to look for the rest of the tourists.

Clint studied the information. Burrows was from California and had been to Canada a year ago when his passport was issued, then he'd just passed through Mexico, Guatemala, Honduras, Nicaragua – where he stayed four days – Costa Rica for two days and here.

Jennifer Clift was from Maryland. She had been in Australia and this trip.

Samuel Keys was from Port King, Australia. He had been to the US (Hawaii and California) and this trip.

Lily Owens was from Carter's Point, Australia. She had been to England and France, then was (reading between the lines) with Keys from that point.

Clint sat back and thought. He had two who could end up with having to explain a thing or two.

Omar came back in with Harry Ammends. The others would come in later. They were pretty much broken up about the death.

"She was deliberately murdered," Clint said. "It doesn't make sense that anyone on the comarca would kill her. That leaves us only a very few suspects. Your group is the most likely. The others didn't know you before here – they claim. If that's not true, we have a prime suspect.

"Did you meet any of them before here?"

"The Aussie group? Sam and Lily are from there so we call them the Aussie group. I don't think so.

Maybe last year in Hawaii. Most surfers end up there at some time or other. Burrows and Clift. I never saw the Aussies before."

"Sandra's passport says she was all over the world where there's good surfing. She could have known all of them I suppose."

"She knew people everywhere we went. It's more than possible. I saw her three or four times in other places back in the states. She went to conventions a lot."

"How are your trips financed?"

"Financed? I'm an advertising idea man. About once a year I get a good one and can relax for awhile. My last commission was more than sixty thou.

"Sandy was trying to get me to use one of her poems in an ad, so she could get royalties. She thought she was a hell of a lot better than she was. Most of her stuff was overdone crap of the most common kind. Blue, coo, true, shoe, glue, you, hue. You don't start trite. You hope your shit will be so repeated that it becomes trite."

"You've all been traveling together since you met in Managua? Your group?"

"Yeah. I'd met Sandy and Gina before. George was with Gina. I'd never met him before. He's a quiet type. I think he resented me for Gina, but she said they were just traveling and weren't into anything serious. Maybe he thought it was more serious."

"You don't seem as broken up about her death as the others."

"I don't think anyone's broken up about it. I was right there when she took the dive. I couldn't tell you what I felt. A little horror. Maybe it was more like I saw a stranger get hit by a bus.

"You know the thing that bothers me? That could have been meant for me. Who knew which kite she would use? Even she didn't until it was time to harness up!"

"The carry harness," Omar replied. "The man's harness is crossover. The woman's harness is square so her tits don't get bruised up."

"Oh. I didn't know there was a way to tell. She slipped into that one so I took the other."

Omar went to get the others. Clint chatted with Harry a bit, then he left. Omar brought Gina Berts in. She said all the novels she read, the detective wanted them separate so they couldn't make up a story when they heard what someone else said.

"Yes," Clint replied. "You had to know Omar would tell me you didn't like her much."

"I despised her. She was nothing but a scheming self-centered bitch! If I'd killed her, it would be with acid dripping into her eyes or something."

"She was that popular with other women?"

"On a good day. That Jim character and Sam Keys didn't see through her. Jenny and Lily took all of five minutes to figure her for what she was. Harry thought she was just over her air head with things and would outlive it. He thought she was just the type that thinks she pisses champagne and shits ice cream. I think George had her sort of figured. He wouldn't get close, but he's the shy type anyway. She would be spouting that awful crap she called poetry and he would be looking at her like he couldn't believe she actually thought it was good. Like he couldn't decide if it was a joke or something.

"Okay. I hated her rotten guts, but I didn't kill her. I thought about it sometimes."

"You'd never met any of the Aussie group before?"

"No. I like them. They're real people."

"Now. When you were all in and around the boat before it left did you see anyone back where the lines were attached to the transom hooks?"

"All of us, I suppose. I wasn't paying much attention. I was concentrating on Omar. Sandy did say he was the best she ever had – and if there was anyone among us who had a thousand ... I'm being catty. That was *her* style, not mine! I get hot around the Indios here. They're gorgeous!"

"That seems to be the consensus. I won't ask if

you think anyone had a reason to kill her."

"Only everybody."

She was leaving when Jenny Clift came to the door.

"Yes?"

"I remembered something that may mean something to you. About the Miller person. I was talking with Lily and Sam. Sandy had met us all, I think. It would be her with a sort of disguise. I remembered because she said something when we met here. She said I had lost a few pounds. I was about ten pounds over what I wanted to be back home about a year ago. Maybe a little more. It was in San Diego. At an international surfer's convention.

"We were in a little place by the beach and she was there with a big yellow straw hat with a lot of drooping hibiscus flowers pinned to it with bright ribbons, mirrored sunglasses, a tie-dyed blouse and a lot of beads. She was reading a poem on a little stage while a guy played a guitar. I remember that they were neither one very good. They came over to our table to sort of try to get donations. We talked and Charlie, the guy I was with, gave them a dollar. Lily and Sam were there and said they thought they saw me on the beach. That made me remember the bad poetry.

"It probably doesn't mean anything, but I didn't

want you to think I was hiding anything. You would find out we were both at that convention I suppose."

"Thanks. As you say, it may not mean anything. If I find that you were there at the same time it would be suspicious, but there are thousands at those conventions. You may have not seen her. It would leave a question."

"That was what I was afraid might happen."

George Peeks came to the door as Jenny left. Clint told him to come on in. He came in and sat.

"Nothing much. Jenny was telling me she met some people at a convention in San Diego and didn't want to leave the impression she was hiding anything.

"Did you meet any of the others here anywhere before this trip?"

"What do you mean? I saw Lily Owens at the convention. Sandy was there acting the space-headed hippie chick. Jim was there. It was close to home for him. Gina, I met in Miami three years ago. Surfers are likely to meet. There aren't a lot of places where the waves are good. We go to things like that. It took every cent I had at the time to get there, but I just *had* to go to that convention!

"It's sort of funny. I worship surfers and the waves. Most of us are very outgoing people. I'm an introvert. I'm more like a groupie than a real surfer, though I really am good.

"It's sort of funny. I won a major competition in Hawaii and no one seemed to even notice. Alan Preston took third place. He was treated like a celebrity.

"It's personality. He even got several bigtime endorsement contracts and I got the one that was part of the prize. It's what pays for me to make these trips. I look good enough for the pictures, but I can't talk and make friends like most others. I'm sort of in the background. At first I didn't like it at all. Now, it's sort of neat. I don't want to be in the spotlight. I'm good and know it. I don't care if no one else does.

"So I'm a liar. I want a few to know. I don't want people pointing at me on the street or in a restaurant and saying he's a big name surfer."

"Do you care that Sandy is dead?"

"Not really. I didn't think too much of her. She always seemed to have a sneaky agenda all the time. It was just a feeling. Women always saw through her right away, but guys usually didn't.

"I had a gay friend – well, more than friend. He took one look at her and said she was about the most scheming bitch he ever saw. She was talking with a guy in a bar and he said her body language and expression were shouting that she was a fraud so loud he couldn't hear what she was saying."

"You're gay?"

"No. Not really. I have a couple of gay friends and find they're more honest than most women. I do enjoy sleeping with them. It's all one way though. They want it that way, too.

"I do all right with the women. I tend to get emotionally involved too fast. I tell them things I regret saying later."

"What did you tell Sandy?"

He sighed. "I met her at that convention and she talked me into playing guitar while she spouted that insipid shit she wrote she thought was the best poetry the world ever saw. I was playing for coins, really. I'm not good at that.

"I told her I'd become so obsessed with going to that convention I'd robbed a convenience store in Rhode Island. She used it to make me play the guitar for her. She tried to use it when I won the competition in Hawaii, but I let her know it was in the past and that I wasn't about to pay anyone any blackmail. She had no proof of anything. It would be her word against mine.

"We sort of got along. I didn't like her and she didn't like me, but there was an understanding."

Clint nodded.

He'd interviewed all of them. He still had a couple of questions he needed answered.

<u>*Q & A*</u>

"What have you learned so far? I'm sending the information by fax for the passports," Generoso said. "You don't have too many suspects, I see. Seven. It should be possible to solve that one easily enough.

"Having said that I laugh cynically."

"I have a couple of suspicions. I've learned a lot about her. I think she was probably blackmailing someone and they grabbed the opportunity to get rid of her where whatever it is won't be exposed. She had blackmailed one person in a minor way before. The type will continue. A lot of them end up dead."

"This is going to be another one where the killer is allowed to go home?"

"It depends on what it was about. Maybe yes, maybe no."

"The passport information won't tell you much. They could have all known each other, perhaps, but it would be for you to determine that."

"They've already said some of them met at a convention and other places. My big question is how did anyone manage to get to that rope with all of them wandering around the boat and area and not be noticed?"

"How long do you estimate it would take?"

"With a good cigarette lighter maybe a minute or two. They would have to be able to explain it. That might pose a problem because none of them smoke. Tobacco. They wouldn't light up a joint out there."

"That would almost mean a distraction. For that little time it wouldn't take much. Something happened that someone else took advantage of or there was a distraction that the one who did it caused."

"How do you figure?"

"It was Maxie's kite boat? He would know everything going on in his boat. Period. You know how careful he is."

"You have a point! I thought of something else that was probably part of it. It may have taken just twenty or thirty seconds. I have to see that rope!"

"Surely you took that evidence and kept it?"

There was silence. Clint finally said, "Shit! I don't believe I didn't ... wait! Maxie!"

"Yes. He will have it. It's his proof he isn't at fault."

The fax machine started printing and Clint rang off. He headed for Maxie's boat. It was still right there on the dock. Maxie wasn't letting anyone get on it. He said he knew Clint would be back for the rope and would want to search the boat and that the tourists had to be questioned right away before they left.

Clint told him the truth. He got in too much of a hurry. He should have stayed on that boat until all the evidence was found.

"No one, and I mean *no one*, has been on the boat since you," Maxie said.

Clint nodded and went aboard. Everything was as he'd left it. He didn't take any evidence, but he had a photographic memory. He'd also used his Blackberry to record everything he'd noted.

He went over the boat by the inch, then to the rope. He used a magnifying glass to check the break. It was what he suspected. Someone was familiar enough with that polypropylene to know just how much to slice through so it would hold until the high twisting stress on the point. The hardening flame balled the ends of the cut fibers.

He had the digital camera and had everything recorded. He unclipped the rope end from the transom ring and cut twenty feet of the broken section above off and put it in an evidence bag – which was a plastic bag from the tienda.

"Maxie, what happened that made you leave the boat for one minute. That's all it took."

"I never leave the boat when we're ready to go

out except to tie and untie ... one minute? When that girl twisted her ankle and dropped all her stuff?

"One of the girls, the blond one, twisted her ankle on the step-up and her bag spilled. I helped her up and she said she was alright. It wasn't sprained. She was just a klutz. She had some stuff in a big handbag that had spread on the dock. I helped pick it all up.

"Clint, it wasn't more than a minute! It was right there on the other side of the dock, maybe eight feet away!"

"The kites were on the rack?"

"Yes. We were ready to go out. We left less than five minutes later."

"So they were between you and the transom for that minute.

"Who was on the boat when she tripped?"

"The Gina girl, the Australian man. We all went to help the girl get up."

"You were all there then. By Lily?"

"The three others were at the end of the dock, taking pictures. The rest were with us and the girl."

Clint looked puzzled a moment, then grinned. "One wasn't.

"Maxie, what kinds of things spilled from that purse?"

"Things? Some suntan lotion. That I remember, because the lid wasn't tight and it leaked a little. It smells like coconut. Let's see. Four or five handkerchiefs, some sunglasses. Keys to the hotel room. A billfold. Two of them. One had credit cards and money and the other identification. Nail clippers. A little plastic packet of pot. Some matches.

"That's all I can remember.

"Help any?"

"Four or five handkerchiefs? They fell out of the bag when she tripped?"

"I see. They were a couple of feet away. They wouldn't have fallen out. They were pulled out. It was an act to get me off the boat."

"I think so. I really think so.

"What connection is there to Australia and the northeast?

"Something's going on here. I have to get that passport information and get on the net. I wonder why they tried to disguise ... I wonder if she had some kind of evidence ... this only adds up one way. Those two are one end. Was she working with someone else? What's it about?"

"Mainly, what are you talking about?" Maxie asked.

"I only have an idea because of what's coming out. Why in hell does this stuff have to come to

Panamá?"

"It's from outside and isn't just someone killing some other person because of personal problems? Just because they're mad ... or that policeman said she was the type who was blackmailing someone. That isn't it?"

"I don't know. She probably was, but not on a personal level. There's something ... Damn it! Matilde saw something in her that was evil! I have to talk with her, then I'm going on the net and staying there until I have an answer or two!"

He took his evidence to the council house and went to find Matilde. She said Miller's aura was all muddy colors and there was too much red. Like there was something between her and the viewer, which mean she was pretending. The red was evil. It wasn't soft red. It was muddy. She was not what she was pretending to be. She was totally evil. Only one of the others was evil. That one was not as evil as Miller. She knew what had happened, but she didn't *directly* kill Miller. The ones who killed her honestly thought they were doing right. No, she wouldn't tell him who killed Miller and, no, she wouldn't say who was evil because it was not a thing from or about the comarca. That evil one had already revealed much. It would be a short time before everyone knew. There would be interference from outside.

Hold great suspicion of all who came to Cusapín in the next two days.

She could see by Clint's demeanor that he knew who killed her. He didn't know what was behind it. It was only partly personal. There was great danger.

Clint was leaving when Matilde called, "Clint! Go home! Now!"

You don't question Matilde about things. Clint broke into a fast run and headed up the beach to his house. There was a boat just coming to the beach below his house. Nito and Nicole were standing on the beach, watching it come in. Clint ran up just as a big man got out and waded to the shore. Nito and Nicole ran to hug Clint. The man came to them to say, "Clint Faraday? I was talking with Judi Lum in Bocas. She asked me to bring you some things."

"Judi? What would she want to send me?"

Judi Lum was Clint's attractive Oriental next door neighbor in Bocas Town who helped him with a lot of his cases. Clint had talked with her on the phone the night before and knew she was in Las Tablas for the past week, not in Bocas Town.

He shrugged and gave Clint a small carved monkey. It was the type of curio Tyna collected.

"Thanks. She knows how Tyna likes these kinds of things. She's given her things she found in other places.

"Would you care for chicha?"

"No thanks. I'm on my way to Colón and told her I'd drop this off.

"This is a beautiful place. I guess it's mostly calm and peaceful. I'm more the money-hungry businessman type. I'd go crazy, but I understand why most people would go for the more tranquil lifestyle where there isn't a lot of what passes for excitement."

"Excitement will come from different things to different people. There's plenty here, but not of the cars and planes and noise and pollution of cities. A big tuna it takes you two hours to tire down. We like little spontaneous fiestas. It's a lot different."

"I suppose you get a lot of surfers. The waves are great here at times I hear."

"Yes. We have a few from Australia and the states here now."

"Oh, yes. That's right. One of them was killed. Murdered?"

"Yeah. I'm investigating it."

"It would be one of them who did it. No Indio would have any reason."

"You'd think so. Two. A third is involved."

He got a hard stare at that!

"Er, I'm Gerry Dell. You caught me! You're

damned sharp! What gave me away?"

"Judi's in Las Tablas and has been for a couple of weeks and she doesn't know how to tell anyone how to get here from the water. She would have you stop in the town to ask for me. You asked questions and made statements that showed you know a hell of a lot about the murder."

"You say two of them killed her and another is involved?"

"Yes."

"And you aren't going to say more."

"Not until I know who you are and what you want here. If you'd gone to town, it would be almost normal, but I suppose one or more of them would recognize you.

"Which government is sponsoring murders and other unpleasant things here?"

"Not governments. Not in a formal sense. An organization that's international. Interpol."

Clint shook his head and took out his phone to call a number he hid from Dell. Manolo, an agent for Interpol answered.

"Gerry Dell," Clint said.

"With?"

"Interpol."

"Fuck no!"

"Thanks." He turned to Dell. "Try again."

Dell shook his head. "So you're a lot more

connected and sharp than they told me. Now you won't believe anything I say."

"Nothing's changed. Try again."

"Can I ask how you knew? You didn't come running up this beach by chance."

"Matilde."

"Who's Matilde?"

"She's the witch woman," Nicole said. "She's never wrong."

"Witch woman?"

"More a medicine woman with a psy talent. She's never wrong. She told Tyna that she was pregnant and that it would be a girl we would name Nicole. Tyna didn't even know she was pregnant at the time. She's always right about those things. She said Miller was evil and that her spirit wouldn't come back when they went out."

"And she told you who killed Miller and that another person was involved."

"No. She told me to come home fast, that there was a threat to my family."

"There was never a threat to your family. Not from here, anyhow!"

"What's in the carving?"

"A very highly sophisticated device that can hear anything within fifty feet or so."

"What's supposed to be said here, for Christ's sake!"

"I haven't a tiny clue. I was told to get it here somehow."

"You don't know what it's about?"

"Will you believe me when I say I don't? It has something to do with a person who sometimes visits you here or something."

"Judi? She's the only one who visits who stays in the house."

"I don't know. I'm to get this thing here – I can imagine we're being monitored right now. I'm to avoid being seen by the surfers and am to go on."

"Nito, tell your mother to come here?"

Nito went to the house. He came back with Tyna about a minute later. Dell was staring at her.

"My god! I can tell that the girl's going to be a knockout! Now I see why! My god! You're beautiful!"

"Oh, you men do go on! What, hon?"

"Matilde said or implied that you and the kids are in danger. It's not from Dell.

"Gerry, my wife, Tyna."

"Danger to us here? On the comarca?" Tyna said. "Someone's living in la-la land!"

"They're professional. I have to know what's going on!

"Here's a little carving, not from Judi. It has a transmitter built in that's reporting this and anything else within twenty meters to someone. I don't believe Dell is the danger, but he might be being used by someone.

"Dell, will you come with me to talk with a witch woman?"

Dell considered a moment. "I think so. I want to know what's going on myself!"

A phone rang in the boat. Dell grinned and went to answer it. Dell yelled, "Down!" Clint threw the carved monkey figure as far as he could into the Caribbean and pulled his family down on the beach. There was an explosion in the air just before the figure hit the water. Dell dove out of the boat.

Dell waded ashore. "Locator."

"And a huge mistake," Clint replied. "I expect to be attacked. It's part of what I do. Attack my family, you've committed suicide!

"Will they have anything on the boat that can report?"

"No. I have a little device that would tell me. They didn't get anything aboard so they won't have any way to tell them they missed. I yanked the radio lead out when I jumped out. I'm just glad that thing didn't carry a bigger charge."

"They aren't too very far to have delivered the missile that fast," Clint said. "We might be seen with opticals.

"Dell, are they big enough to be watching us

from a satellite right now?"

"Oh, yeah! We can hope they didn't think of that."

"They will. Let's move fast. The newer opticals can show them the pores on our faces if they're focused on us."

They all ran up the beach and into the house. There was a good chance they had a few minutes. They wouldn't be on the beach. The boat would be there. The explosion was close enough that it made a shock wave that could have knocked them down from the distance.

Clint thought, then told Dell to come with him. They only had seconds, if that!

They ran to the little palm frond shelter by the beach. Clint waved to come on and he and Dell hit the center pole, knocking the shelter down. Clint used a lighter to set the fronds afire. They went back to the house.

"If they use the satellite, they'll think we were in the hut. The missile hit it. We're no longer a problem," Clint explained.

"But we are!" Dell snarled. "That was meant to take me out with you!"

"We're a problem beyond anything they ever dreamed of!" Tyna said. "I'm exactly like Clint there! Attack me, okay. Attack my family, be sure your funeral is paid in advance!"

<u>*Tag! You're It!*</u>

"Oh, hell!" Clint said as several people came running along the beach from the town. "They heard the explosion."

Omar came to look at the house. They all saw the frond hut was burning and ran to it. Clint and Gerry were in the trees by the beach and caught Omar's eye. He waved to stay silent and get the others away. He pointed to the boat.

Jenny Clift was with them. The rest there were Indios.

Omar yelled for them to check the boat. He was going to check the house. He ran toward the house and Jenny led the bunch to the boat. She had her cell phone held out, though the water was only about two feet deep at the front of the boat. She was obviously taking a video of the scene. She carefully swept over the boat as she climbed aboard to look in the cabin.

She came back out to say there was no one there. She then started speaking into the phone – without punching a number, meaning she had been sending the whole bit to someone.

"Matilde said there was another who was evil,

but not as bad as Miller," Clint whispered to Gerry, pointing to Jenny. "Tag! You're it!

"What's ... we can't risk talking here."

Gerry nodded and silently went deeper into the copse. Omar came from the house, calling that no one was there. Maybe they all went up into the mountains and something somebody left in the shelter exploded. Maybe extra gasolene for the boat that wasn't vented and got hot. Clint had an idea and waved for him to draw them away somehow.

Nito and Nicole had been playing on the beach and had gone up and down several times since there was anything that would erase footprints. Omar pointed to the ones going on up the beach and said maybe they went to the stream to show a gringo friend where Dave had planted the orchids. He started running up the beach and the rest followed. Jenny obviously didn't want to, but she had little choice if she was to appear to be with them to see that Clint and family were alright. Clint ran to the house as soon as they were far enough away and to the little bodega. He was under tree cover all the way from above. They wouldn't have to worry about possible satellite observation. He found what he was looking for and spewed the contents around, then smashed the can with a handy rock. He pulled the rupture outward and poured a little gasolene on it, took it to the burning shelter and threw it in where it almost exploded.

"What was that about?" Gerry asked. He had come back to watch. "They're coming back."

"Omar's smart. He'll see what I'm doing and will handle it."

"Okay. What was the can?"

"Starting fluid. Ether."

"And there was a little rock cooker thing about where you tossed it. Will he catch it?"

"I think so." They stepped back into the copse to be completely out of sight. Omar saw when Clint waved a small piece of white cloth and pointed to the shelter. He made a motion like he was using hair spray or something in a spray can.

Omar didn't seem to react at all. He talked with the group on the beach a moment, then went to the shelter, which was now just a few ashes. He saw the burned ether can and yelled that he found what caused the explosion and fire. Starting fluid. Maybe their guest from the boat didn't know how to use it and left it sitting too close to the oven. It overheated and the can ruptured, or maybe the plastic nozzle burned off. Boom!

They were obviously not there. They'd probably gone out in another boat. Tuna were running. Gringos liked to catch them. There was no one there when that can exploded or there would be a body. The Faradays and guests would probably come home that afternoon and be pissed as hell because their sun shelter had burned down!

They all went on up the beach toward Cusapín. Clint and Gerry went to the house. Tyna and the kids were talking with Matilde. She had come through the forest on her horse. She said she was in time and knew Clint and the family were safe now, but not for long. There was great danger from someone very powerful in money somewhere else.

Clint pointed to Gerry. She said he was hiding a lot, but some of it from himself. He was not a bad person and was not evil. He was very much being used by evil people.

"What's it about? Do you know?" Clint asked.

"No. It's about a lot of money and more about power. It's about ... your friend, Dave?"

"Is there any connection you can see with Darien?" Clint asked.

She looked thoughtful and said, "Yes, but also other places and a secret that was more powerful than all of the evil ones behind this. It was a thing they feared."

Clint looked grim. "This is a very hard question. Is it something that doesn't exist now, but that has existed in the past and could exist in the future?"

"That is a very complicated question. I think it does not exist now. They fear that it can exist tomorrow. It can take their power away from them, if it is ... used. It can take their power away from them if it's not used?

"It is a thing that can take all power away from everyone, but give the holder absolute power if it is used only as a threat?

"Clint, you bring some very strange things to life. We have no reason to fear it here on the comarca. Most of the rest of the world ... no. Only the ... large places with large cities and ... transportation?"

"I may know what it is. You know Dave. This is as stupid as anything they ever did.

"Gerry, we have to stop this!"

"You said Darien? It has something to do with that plan to move oil tankers overland?"

"Indirectly. Someone mentioned that?"

"I overheard a conversation on shortwave radio. Something about how that project was stopped. Something about a couple of Indios who had brought the entire government to its knees."

"Do they have sense enough to not confront Dave directly?"

"Who is this Dave? They're pretty savvy. The Indios have brought the government to their knees two or three times. The big bad modern warfare with direction from the satellites we're hiding from now is meaningless to the people on the comarcas and in the jungles. The Nicaragua thing proved that.

"Oh. It's something that ... it doesn't make sense. The satellites aren't any good for that, so shutting them down wouldn't mean much."

"It could probably shut them down. That would end communications for a lot of places," Clint said. "The net would be through, for the most part. That would make your employers happy, but it would also end their control of banking and business."

"I see what this lady means about transportation! GPS locators are used in everything from planes to trucks on the highway to ships ... Christ! If you shut down the satellites modern civilization collapses in a couple of days without a shot being fired!

"It can't be laser. The Indios couldn't build them. It's something they can build!"

"From what he's said to me it's something a ten year old kid could build with things around the house," Tyna said. "This is all so interesting, but it doesn't do anything for our situation.

"Clint, warn Dave!"

Clint took out his (satellite!) phone to call Dave, who didn't answer. He tried twice again and was answered.

"Dave, there's a situation here that puts you and all of us in danger. It's about the thing you let the Indios use in Darien with that stupid land route thing. I thought you should be warned. Some very powerful people, according to Matilde, want to get their hands on it. They don't care how."

"What? They're that stupid? You know damned well anyone could make one. They make one, then their enemies make one, then you have a situation with an inevitable outcome. Chaos!"

"They probably haven't considered that point," Gerry said (it was on speaker). "I think they want to invent a counter."

"Dave, Gerry," Clint introduced.

"It's not counterable. It's true mutually assured destruction. By that I mean if they get it they're assured they'll all be destroyed. They've kicked around too many millions of people for too long. All sides of it. There'll be, in a word, terrible retribution against all.

"Hell! I'll put on the web how to make the thing! We won't be affected much here."

"You're on the comarca?" Tyna asked.

"In the mountains inland. I'm with friends a little north of Piedra Roja."

"I'll try to get the message to them that they'd better consider that they can't defend and that once one is built everyone will have it," Gerry said. "They tried to take me out with Clint and family. If I wasn't afraid it would cost me as much as them I'd say to put it on the web!"

"It wouldn't affect you much if you stayed on the comarca."

"I couldn't stand the quiet life. I..."

"Someone evil comes!" Matilde said, sharply.

"It would be Jenny," Clint said. "We'll be in touch." He rang off. Everyone moved to where they couldn't be seen from outside. Jenny came striding up the path from the beach. She called, "Faraday!"

Clint went to the door and stepped out on the porch. "What?"

"We have to talk. This thing's gotten a long way out of hand.

"And I'm the cause of that?"

"Some of the people involved are too used to giving orders and having them followed. They feel invulnerable.

"We're all vulnerable. One button gets pushed and everyone within a hundred meters of that house cease to be a problem anymore."

"What? You're so stupid you threaten me after what's already gone down?"

"I'm delivering a message."

"You've got somebody listening?"

"Certainly!"

"Good. Anything happens to my family, Dave, me or my people and a diagram and instructions go on the net worldwide to fifty three sites that are used by more than seven million people in every country you can name. A majority of those people do *not* like your associates even a little bit. They find themselves in what seems a hopeless situation because of them. They'll demand full retribution. A lot of them don't like each other so it will extend to that, but your associates will be first priority. There won't be business as usual ever again. For a long time there won't be any business at all. Civilization as we know it will collapse. Totally."

"To hear the propaganda. I don't think you can do anything."

"Then why are you here?"

"I didn't say that none of them feel that way. They're the bosses."

"What did Miller have to do with this crap?"

"Nothing. Some of the group didn't like her. I despised her. I helped plan that. We didn't take you into consideration. We didn't know you were here. I didn't. They probably never heard of you."

"Well, tell your bosses that any other crap out of them and I'm here on the comarca. Nothing much will be affected here. Seventy five percent of the world couldn't survive here, even though the food and basics we need are here. Food will stop going to the cities. Fuel will stop going to the cities. People won't be able to travel except on horseback or walking. The reason Dave hasn't already put this on the web is that in Mexico City alone more than four million people would starve within a few weeks. Think of New York, Los Angeles, Rio, the big cities all over the world. No power. No means of escaping. No food. No water. No nothing!

"Dave's where you can't get close to him. It can't be stopped if it starts. They'd better think about that! You can't unsing a song!"

Matilde stepped out behind him. "There are three coming in a boat."

"They are evil?" Clint asked.

"They are them. They are not consciously evil as is this one. It is what they know. They are products of their society and upbringing. They are truly dangerous, but more to themselves than to you. They are not unintelligent. You can convince them of truth.

"I will return to Cusapín."

She whistled. A few seconds later her horse came around the house. She mounted and rode away.

"She thinks I'm consciously evil?"

"She knows. That's Matilde. She's never been known to be wrong.

"Who's coming?"

"You've got me! I doubt anyone is."

"Bet? Say five thousand dollars?"

They saw a small dot on the water toward Chiriui Grande. It was a fast boat and was there very quickly. It stopped just out from Gerry's boat. There were three men in it. One was in a darkbusiness suit. A very expensive business suit.

"Does something seem out of place here to you?" Clint asked. Jenny hid a grin.

The men argued a moment, then the larger one took the one in a suit on his back and waded to shore where the suit dismounted and walked carefully across the sand to the path to the house. Clint stood there watching, amusement all over his face. Tyna rolled her eyes and went inside.

"You should have a dock built. I'm Gilbert T. Samuelson the fourth." In European English.

"I'm just Clint. We don't usually have visitors from the water and they come in bathing suits anyhow. I think that'll be the first suit anyone around here ever saw around here. You're a mite overdressed."

Nito came out and looked at the man standing there. He turned to his father and said, "Who's the doofus in a suit?" in English. "Mom says if these people are staying for dinner she has to kill another chicken."

Samuelson laughed. "I'm used to wearing a business suit to make an impression, son."

"You made one, but not the one you wanted to." Nito answered. "You impressed me that you don't know anything about the comarca. You have to be another one of those cruds who come here to try to screw the Indios out of their land so you can make a lot of money you can use to make a lot more to use to make more. Sort of pointless.

"They staying for dinner, Dad?"

"No."

He went back inside. Samuelson shook his head and laughed again. "What is he? Six years old? He sounds like my fifty year old brother!

"He had me pegged, I think. I'm not trying to get your land. I'm trying to find out if the stories I've heard about a super weapon the Indios have is real or fantasy."

"It's real, but they don't have it now. They can have it when and if they need it. You heard what we've said already."

"Some others have, perhaps. Miss Clift does not work for my group. No one in my group would take the chances those are taking. If this is real, it could lead to disaster!

"Have you seen any physical demonstration of

the weapon? You can say that it's largely as presented?"

"I saw a couple of things where it was used. All I can say is that a plane was shot down with it at a distance of several kilometers. The shot went through several metal reinforcement bars. It didn't expand. It made a perfect hole."

"It is not a laser?"

"Not as I understand it. It fires a projectile of some sort."

"A very hard metal, perhaps?"

"A child's marble, perhaps. It looks like the projectile was that size. Dave once picked a few up on the street in Bocas and said it was hard to believe that something like that could go through an armored tank."

"A child's marble? Glass?"

"It's a matter of velocity. His little invention seems to move it at a good percent of the speed of light. Dave says it could be made of balsa wood. At that speed it would go through armored steel."

"But ... how would you be able ... I don't know how you could supply the energy to accelerate anything to that speed!"

"You just put it in a different time base. Time affects velocity. I don't begin to understand it. I know it works."

"What...?"

"You put it into a more compressed time base that's affecting this one. It's something to do with a background time that makes it possible to have several time bases ... I don't have any idea what I'm saying. Dave says it's simple and something that's been around a long time. It has something to do with what he calls a gyroscopic effect."

"All I want to know is how to defend against it, personally."

"You can't."

"They took Clift with them?" Gerry asked.

"Yeah. I think she didn't want to go, but they took her," Clint answered. "I think they're very interested in finding just who she works for. That turkey was really terrified of what they could cause to start here. I wonder if Dave really has something that easy ... well, the Indios in Darien made a couple so he does."

"What's the threat? I know they feel it's real and they're the target."

"The threat is that Dave really will put it on the net if they don't back off of certain practices. If it's true that it only uses a few things laying around the house and that a ten year old can make one, think of what will happen when any nutcase or terrorist can make one. Would you want to get on a plane? If you're in a big city that depends on food coming from outside and those people can stop it from coming? In the slums of Rio or Mexico City or Los Angeles? If they could stop fuel from being delivered and could hole every transformer at any major electric plant? If they could hole the pumps that send water to your city?

"It's damned scary!"

"And the people in these jungles wouldn't even know about it while civilization comes to a halt. It's more than scary!

"It's true that he has the data on fifty some-odd websites, ready for release?"

"I doubt it. He'll have it on some. I just came up with a number. All it takes is one.

"You know what else is weird and scary?"

"What? Besides that Matilde woman. She's not a hag. She's rather pretty. She's not over thirty five. She can read minds or something."

"No. She feels things, but doesn't read minds. She knows if you're lying, always, and she has premonitions. She's always right. It's some kind of psy power.

"What gets me is that a murder that didn't have anything to do with this caused it to happen."

"I don't believe that. The Miller woman had something huge to do with it. They grabbed an opportunity to get rid of her. Clift was lying when she said it didn't have anything to do with it. She was from the northeast United States. So was Miller. That can't be that much of a coincidence."

"True. And she was into blackmail. Maybe she had the goods on someone. On the wrong one."

"It occurs to me."

They talked about it for awhile longer, then used

Gerry's boat to go into Cusapín where Clint found the surfers were impatient to leave. He said they could go, even Lily and George, who had gotten rid of Sandy. He knew they were drawn into that. Jenny wasn't around. She caught a ride to Chiriqui Grande with some people in a boat.

He learned that a couple had come to spend a day or two in Cusapín. They were from France. They were the very wealthy type who were not too bad. A little prone to give orders and expect city services here in the comarca. Their name was LeGrande.

Clint saw a studied look on Gerry's face and said now was the time to lay it on the line. If he knew something, now was the time.

"The name's familiar. It's in my group. Now I wonder about a few more things."

"Like the fact you were in communication with them when they sent that missile to get rid of all of us?"

"That, too."

Gerry booked a room at the hotel where Andrea and Liam LeGrande were staying. They managed to be crossing the lobby when Clint and Gerry came in. She showed a little shock. He flickered, but didn't show any real reaction.

"Ah! Dell, wasn't it? We met in Mexico City last fall?"

"Yes, but it was just last week. This is Clint Faraday. He was supposed to have been blown up with me. You missed.

"I think we should have a little talk."

LeGrande stared at him, then turned to Clint. He shrugged and waved to a sofa to one side. Andrea said she had a headache and would go to their room for some Tylenol. Clint and Gerry sat on the sofa. LeGrande pulled up a stool by the door so that he was sitting high and looking down on them. Clint grinned at him.

"The psychological crap won't work on the comarca. It'll just give you an uncomfortable seat," Clint said. "I've heard enough crap about weapons and that shit. Lay it on the line. What did she have on you?"

"She? Who?"

"Sandy Miller."

"I don't know any Sandy Miller. If you mean Olga Prednokov, who was killed while using a name of the type, she was infiltrating a group who are working to consolidate an international banking system that is critical for today's world. She found some information that will prove very damaging to several of the people concerned.

"We are deeply concerned about that supposed weapon. I do not believe it exists personally, but the threat of such a thing is immense."

"It exists. It was stupid as all hell to bring this operation here!" Gerry said. "Other pressures can bring Panamá in without that kind of idiocy.

"Clint, I'm a bit more than someone hired by them. I truly believe that an international, a world money system, is vital to the future. I'm not really someone who's in the core, but I am in. I'm here because of the weapon. What Sandy Miller might have had, I never had a clue. What Prednokov had I know about. It has to do with the consolidation of the European and Chinese influences. She had things that would put them at cross-purposes. She had recordings of meetings among a small group, the ones we've been fighting, discussing how to draw China in, then make them into a secondary influence.

"She'll have arranged for the recordings to be released if anything happens to her. She was a long way from stupid."

"Maybe she was. Maybe we found it and a way to counter it," LeGrand said with a smirk.

"How did you manage to engineer that kiting accident? Clift?" Clint asked.

"No. We let her make the plan and used our own person to work it."

"Peeks?" Clint asked.

"Yes. He's a very good agent. He's the type who you don't notice while he's standing right in front of you."

"Which is how I figured him from the first," Clint agreed. "I let them all go. I imagine you'll have gotten him out of the country by now."

"Yes. He was in Costa Rica less than half an hour ago. There is no one here they can use to connect me."

"Yes there is," Gerry said.

"You? I think not! You have proof of nothing!"

"No. Me," Clint said. "You just sat there and confessed."

"It's your word against mine. I'm one of the world's most respected businessmen."

"And I'm the law here on the comarca. You have just officially confessed to hiring a murder on the comarca so come under comarca law. I am that law at the moment. You are found guilty. You will serve six years at hard labor here on the comarca.

"Next case!"

Gerry was looking greatly amused. LeGrand was looking a little more than scared.

"I ... I must consult with a lawyer! You can't do this!"

"Denied. I can and did do this. The council will have to approve, but it's as good as done."

Omar came in. Clint told him to lock LeGrand in the holding cell, the only one in the town, until they could arrange something. He would be in the fields tomorrow. Start him with yuca, then corn, then plaintains. They would have to work out some kind of schedule. He would be there for six years.

"I hope he has better work clothes than those!" Omar cried. "My god! They won't hold up an hour!"

"Yes. I suppose he has the money to buy some sturdy work clothes. He's not used to working. You'll have to show him what to do and how to do it.

"Gerry, maybe you can tell the Mrs. what has transpired?"

Gerry nodded, grinned, and went to the stairs. Omar told LeGrand to come along. LeGrand said he wasn't going anywhere. Omar said he had experience with bigshit non-Indio businessmen. He could expect to be treated the way he treated others. If he cooperated, things would be easy. If not, they would be a long way from pleasant. LeGrand looked completely bewildered as Omar led him out.

Andrea and Gerry came flying into the lobby. She was screeching that the LeGrands were not going to be treated like the trash these savages were used to being around! And where was her husband? Did they have any idea who he *was*?!

"He's a man who hired a murder. He is just another person on the comarca, no better and not much worse than anyone else. He has committed a crime. He was found guilty and will serve five years working in the fields. You obviously can afford to find a place here or you can go back home or whatever."

"But he wasn't ever given a trial and doesn't have a lawyer here!" she cried. "You can't just make up laws as you go!"

"I can, but this is an old law. He admitted to the court that he hired a murder. The law says five years working in the fields if there was possibly justification or as much as death if there wasn't. The court found there was some so he got a minimum sentence," Clint said. "You can argue with the council when Chief Basilio gets back. Probably in a day or two.

"I recommend that you approach it only as a question of whether I followed the law. If you protest beyond that they'll investigate. They could well find that I was too easy and add time to the sentence."

Gerry was looking amused again. She was aghast.

"How much?" she asked, suddenly.

"How much what?" Clint replied.

"To let him go."

"Three billion dollars."

"That's insane! In France it would be fifty thousand Euros!"

"In case you didn't notice, this ain't France," Gerry said. "Clint, do you really want him here?"

"Of course not, but it's the law."

"Can you have him transferred to Chiriqui or somewhere?"

"Buabidi. On the comarca. They could arrange for him to be sent to the Chiriqui facility, I suppose."

"Do that!" Andrea cried. "Maybe they'll be more ... practical."

Clint shrugged. He told them he would contact Basilio as soon as he came back and see if that would be best for everyone. They weren't really set up for this kind of thing.

"He'll be back here in a day or two. We'll see what he says," Clint promised. She looked triumphant. Gerry looked bewildered. She headed back to her room and Gerry asked what he was doing.

"I think three days of hard labor for someone who never lifted a pinkie for anything before might make him think a bit. I'll see that the guys make him bust his ass! He's found a place where his money and power are nothing more than a bad joke."

"I see what you're doing. Make him live the way he's forcing millions of people to live for a few days. See if that makes him a little more careful."

"I think Basilio will be back in two days. He'll negotiate with the capital of the comarca for two more, then LeGrand can be shackled and sent to Buabidi. They can hold him in a cell there with people his policies have made desperate, then sent to Chiriqui where he'll drop a few thousand and go home. He'll be another one where it's a lot easier and much cheaper to make leave the country than to incarcerate for years. He'll be another bigshot billionaire who's persona non grata in Panamá."

"That'll get to her. Not to him. He'll steam, but he's really scared of that weapon. He'll keep shut up."

"Yeah. I'm going back home. I'll leave Omar instructions to see that LePoof gets a little lesson in life."

Clint wrote a note and went home. Tyna said he was getting into a habit of finding weird people in weirder situations. He agreed.

"So what happened then?" Dave asked. They were sitting on Clint's porch having a guanabana chicha. LeGrand and murder were a month in the past.

"Basilio came back home in three more days and made arrangements to transfer him to Buabidi. That took four more days. LePoof had blisters on his hands that Matilde treated. Madam LePoof went to David to wait until he was transferred there. It cost her sixty grand to have him expelled from the country," Clint reported. "Gerry Dell went back to Europe to work on the world bank idea. I don't know if I like the idea or not. It's inevitable, I suppose."

Dave nodded. "It's inevitable. It's a good idea, but not with that crowd running things. No one will be free again. They'll control the economy of the entire world. Only places like the comarca will be unconcerned and they'll probably try to take them over with armed forces."

"Which your weapon will prevent?"

"If it comes to that, everything's over. It'll be another thing where the entire world will be affected except for the places like this. The cities will become what those overdone SciFi action movies predict. Gangs of kill-crazy punks."

"Well, it won't be like those stupid things where monster insects come across space in modern super-science spaceships to try to kill off everyone here. I mean, they're intelligent enough to build those ships, but are nothing but insects? Gimme a break!" Nito said.

"Well, we've had enough of that kind of thing. The weird thing is how Clint seems to have that stuff follow

him everywhere," Tyna said.

"Too true. So how's the tuna run?" Dave asked. It was time to get back to the real world.

C. D. Moulton's works are available on most major outlets as printed or e-books. CD writes the CD Grimes, PI, mysteries, the Det. Lt. Nick Storie mysteries, the Clint Faraday mysteries, the Flight of the Maita science fiction series, books on orchid culture and many others of many types. Mystery, adventure, intrigue, science fiction, humor, fantasy, paranormal, mild erotica, and factual.